A Merry-Mouse
Book of Nursery Rhymes

PRISCILLA HILLMAN

Doubleday & Company, Inc.
Garden City, New York

A Merry-Mouse
Book of
Nursery Rhymes

To My Mother

Designed by Marilyn Schulman

Library of Congress Catalog Card Number 80-2053
ISBN: 0-385-17102-1 Trade
ISBN: 0-385-17103-X Prebound

Jack Be Nimble

Jack be nimble,
   Jack be quick,
      Jack jump over
         The candlestick.

Ladybug, Ladybug

Ladybug, Ladybug
Fly away home,
Your house is on fire
And your children all gone;
All except one
And that's little Ann
And she has crept under
The warming pan.

Jack and Jill

Jack and Jill went up the hill
To fetch a pail of water;
Jack fell down and broke his crown,
And Jill came tumbling after.

Little Jack Horner

Little Jack Horner
Sat in the corner,
Eating a Christmas pie;
He put in his thumb,
And pulled out a plum,
And said, "What a good boy am I!"

Hickory Dickory Dock

Hickory, dickory, dock,
The mouse ran up the clock.
The clock struck one,
The mouse ran down,
Hickory, dickory, dock.

See-Saw, Margery Daw

See-saw, Margery Daw,
    Jacky shall have a new master;
        He shall have but a penny a day,
            Because he can't work any faster.

Mistress Mary, Quite Contrary

Mistress Mary, quite contrary
How does your garden grow?
With silver bells and cockle shells,
And pretty maids all in a row.

London Bridge Is Falling Down

London Bridge is falling down,
Falling down, falling down,
London Bridge is falling down,
My fair lady.

Build it up with wood and clay,
Wood and clay, wood and clay,
Build it up with wood and clay,
My fair lady.

Little Miss Muffet

Little Miss Muffet
Sat on a tuffet,
Eating her curds and whey;
Along came a spider,
And sat down beside her,
And frightened Miss Muffet away.

The Old Woman
Who Lived in a Shoe

There was an old woman who lived in a shoe,
She had so many children she didn't know what to do;
She gave them some broth without any bread;
She spanked them all soundly and put them to bed.

Peter, Peter, Pumpkin Eater

Peter, Peter, pumpkin eater,
Had a wife and couldn't keep her.
He put her in a pumpkin shell
And there he kept her very well.

Hot Cross Buns

Hot cross buns!
Hot cross buns!
One a penny, two a penny,
Hot cross buns!

If you haven't any daughters
Give them to your sons.
One a penny, two a penny,
Hot cross buns!

Pat-a-Cake, Pat-a-Cake

Pat-a-cake, pat-a-cake, baker's man,
Bake me a cake as fast as you can.
Pat it and prick it, and mark it with B
And put it in the oven for baby and me.

Diddle, Diddle, Dumpling

Diddle, diddle, dumpling, my son John
Went to bed with his trousers on.
One shoe off, and one shoe on,
Diddle, diddle, dumpling, my son John.

Little Tommy Tittlemouse

Little Tommy Tittlemouse
Lived in a little house.
He caught fishes
In other men's ditches.

One, Two, Three, Four

One, two, three, four
Mary at the cottage door.
Five, six, seven, eight
Eating cherries off a plate.

Hush, Baby, My Doll

Hush, baby, my doll, I pray you don't cry,
And I'll give you some bread and some milk by and by.
Or, perhaps, you like custard, or, maybe, a tart—
Then to either you're welcome, with all my whole heart.

Jack Sprat and His Wife

Jack Sprat could eat no fat,
    His wife could eat no lean,
        And so between them both, you see,
        They licked the platter clean.

Ride a Cock-Horse

Ride a cock-horse to Banbury Cross
To see a fine lady upon a white horse;
Rings on her fingers and bells on her toes,
And she shall have music wherever she goes.

I Had a Little Hobby Horse

I had a little hobby horse
And it was dapple gray,
Its head was made of pea-straw,
Its tail was made of hay.

I sold him to an old woman
For a copper groat
And I'll not sing my song again
Without a new coat.

A Diller, A Dollar

A diller, a dollar,
   A ten o'clock scholar,
      What makes you come so soon?
         You used to come at ten o'clock,
         But now you come at noon.

Little Betty Blue

Little Betty Blue
Lost her holiday shoe,
What can little Betty do?
Give her another
To match the other
And then she may walk out in two.

A Candle

Little Nancy Etticoat,
With a white petticoat,
And a red nose;
She has no feet or hands,
The longer she stands
The shorter she grows.

Rock-a-Bye Baby

Rock-a-bye baby in the treetop,
When the wind blows the cradle will rock.
When the bough breaks, the cradle will fall,
And down will come baby, cradle and all.

Pease Porridge Hot

Pease porridge hot,
Pease porridge cold,
Pease porridge in the pot
Nine days old.

Some like it hot,
Some like it cold,
Some like it in the pot
Nine days old.

Rub-a-Dub-Dub

Rub-a-dub-dub,
  Three men in a tub;
    And who do you think they be?
      The butcher, the baker,
        The candlestick maker.
          Turn 'em out, Knaves all three!

Twinkle, Twinkle, Little Star

Twinkle, twinkle, little star,
   How I wonder what you are,
     Up above the world so high
      Like a diamond in the sky.
       Twinkle, twinkle, little star,
        How I wonder what you are.